Text copyright © 2021 Harold Grinspoon Foundation
Illustration copyright © 2021 Sally Walker

Published in 2022 by PJ Publishing

PJ Publishing, an imprint of PJ Library, creates board books, picture books, chapter books, and graphic novels that represent the diversity of Jewish families today. By sharing Jewish narratives, values, and life events, we help families explore their connections with Jewish life. In addition to our many English-language titles, we also publish in German, Portuguese, Russian, Spanish, and Ukrainian.

For information regarding permissions, please email permissions@hgf.org or contact us at the address listed below.

PJ Library, a program of the Harold Grinspoon Foundation
67 Hunt Street, Suite 100
Agawam, MA 01001 USA

Library of Congress Control Number: 2021945726

Designed by Michael Grinley

First Edition
10 9 8 7 6 5 4 3 2 1
0522/B1870/A6
Printed in China

Until the
Blueberries
Grow

Written by Jennifer Wolf Kam
Illustrated by Sally Walker

Ben's great-grandpa, Zayde, was moving away.

"Ben," Zayde said. "This house doesn't fit me anymore. I need a smaller space."

Ben took Zayde's hand. "Zayde, stay until the blueberries grow."

Zayde squeezed Ben's hand. "I can stay in this big house a little longer," he said. "Until the blueberries grow."

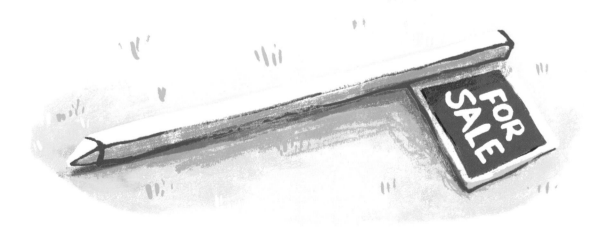

The summer grass tickled Ben and Zayde's feet.
They plucked fat blueberries from the bushes
and squished them between their fingers.
They popped the blueberries into their mouths,
and the juice dribbled down their chins.

"It's hot as horseradish out here," said Zayde.

Ben poured Zayde a glass of water. "Zayde, stay until the grapes are ripe."

Zayde drank the water. "The autumn winds will cool things down. I'll stay until the grapes are ripe."

Ben and Zayde draped bunches of grapes around the sukkah.
Others, they boiled in pots until the kitchen smelled of sweet jelly.

Zayde made Ben a jelly sandwich; then they
stomped through crisp autumn leaves.

"So many leaves!" said Zayde.
"What will we do with them all?"

Ben gathered an armful.
"Zayde, stay until the snow falls."

"There's no yard work in the
winter," Zayde said. "I'll stay
until the snow falls."

A downy blanket of snow covered Zayde's yard. Ben and Zayde tasted tingly snowflakes, and Ben rolled down the hill until he was dizzy.

Zayde wrapped Ben in a quilt and made him a mug of hot chocolate. They lit the chanukkiah and munched latkes and jelly donuts.

"This is fun," said Zayde. "But winter in this big house is hard on these old bones."

Ben placed a sweater on Zayde's shoulders, and they sat together beside the glowing candles.

"Zayde, stay until the flowers bloom."

"The spring sun will warm things up," said Zayde. "I'll stay until the flowers bloom."

Ben and Zayde picked tulips and placed them on the seder table.

Ben found the afikomen in the lilac bushes.

After the Seder, Ben and Zayde curled up under the magnolia tree, and the gentle spring breeze rocked them to sleep.

That night, Zayde held on to the railing. "The staircase is very tall."

Ben took Zayde's hand. "Stay."

Zayde squeezed Ben's hand.

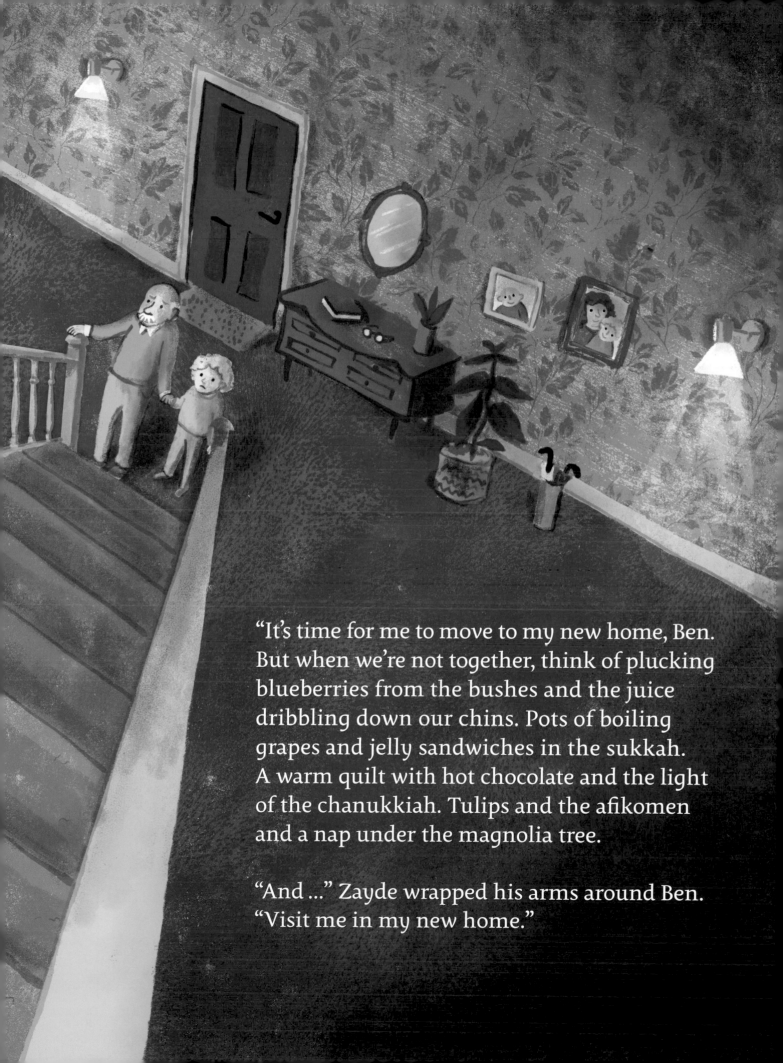

"It's time for me to move to my new home, Ben. But when we're not together, think of plucking blueberries from the bushes and the juice dribbling down our chins. Pots of boiling grapes and jelly sandwiches in the sukkah. A warm quilt with hot chocolate and the light of the chanukkiah. Tulips and the afikomen and a nap under the magnolia tree.

"And ..." Zayde wrapped his arms around Ben. "Visit me in my new home."

When Zayde moved, Ben visited.

"Such a fancy new home, Ben," said Zayde.
"It's like a hotel."

Ben placed a basket on Zayde's lap.
"For you."

"Blueberries! Thank you."

Zayde popped a blueberry into his mouth.
Then another. Ben did the same.

"Stay until we eat *all* of the blueberries?" said Zayde.

"Yes, Zayde," said Ben. "I'll stay."